To Mum, Dad, Ellie and Laura – C.M.

To Simon, for all your help
over the years – R.M.

First published in Great Britain in 2010 by
Piccadilly Press,
A Templar/Bonnier publishing company
Deepdene Lodge, Deepdene Avenue,
Dorking, Surrey, RH5 4AT
www.piccadillypress.co.uk

Text © Ciaran Murtagh, 2010
Illustrations © Richard Morgan, 2010
Cover illustration by Garry Davies
Author photograph by Steve Ullathorne

ISBN: 978 1 84812 058 7

3 5 7 9 10 8 6 4

Printed in the UK by CPI Group (UK) Ltd, Croydon, CR0 4YY

DINOPOO

Ciaran Murtagh

Illustrated by Richard Morgan

Piccadilly

CHAPTER 1

The teeth of the T. Rex glistened in the early morning light. They were smeared with blood and bits of fur. The T. Rex kicked away a pile of bones that were all that remained of his breakfast, and growled. From his home, high up on the mountain, it looked as if he could crush the tiny town of Sabreton with one stamp of his enormous foot. He sharpened his claws against the walls of his cave, let out an ear-splitting cry, and stomped down the mountain. It was time to find Charlie Flint.

It was another lovely morning in Sabreton. The stone buildings shone gold in the bright summer sunshine and the dusty high street was bustling with dinosaurs and people. The Hungry Bone Café was packed with customers ordering breakfast. Charlie Flint smiled as he watched Peter Tray, the waiter, totter between tables, placing plates of scrambled pterodactyl eggs and mammoth-meat sausages in front of eager, hungry faces.

'Morning, Charlie!' called Peter with a wave. 'What dinopants are you making today?'

Since the invention of dinopants, everyone in Sabreton knew Charlie Flint. He had come up with the idea of dinopants to stop dinosaurs pooing in the street. He realised that if dinosaurs had a reason to think before they pooed then they might be more considerate about where they did it. The dinosaurs loved to wear their pants and now they always pooed in Dinopoo Field. Charlie had solved Sabreton's dinopoo problem. But it wasn't just the dinosaurs of Sabreton that wore dinopants any more. Charlie's reputation had spread far and wide and dinosaurs came from all over the land to buy pairs for themselves.

Charlie even had his own dinopants shop at the end of the high street. On most days there was a long queue of dinosaurs waiting patiently outside, eager to be fitted for a pair.

Charlie looked up at the sun. He was late. He wanted to do a bit of extra work in the shop before heading to school that morning, so he began to run.

When he got to the shop, Billy 'The Boulder' Blackfoot had already started getting out their bone and stone tools.

'Sorry I'm late,' said Charlie as he rushed inside.

Billy rolled his eyes and nudged Charlie playfully on the back before getting up from his workbench. Billy, who was one of Charlie's best friends, helped out at the dinopants shop every day. He was very tall for his age and had massive muscles on his arms and legs. His strength made him a natural when it came to cutting up animal skins, but despite his tough-guy looks, Billy was one of the nicest people in Sabreton.

When the dinosaurs came to the shop, Charlie would measure them up and design a pair of dinopants for them. Then the dinosaurs picked out the colours they wanted and Billy chopped up the right amount of animal skin. Charlie's other best friend, James Tusk, carefully stitched everything together with a bone needle and thread. The shop doubled as the boys' workshop and tools littered the three wooden workbenches at the back of the room.

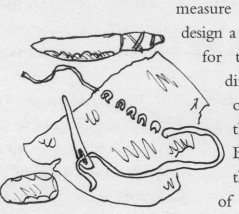

Billy picked a bright blue fur skin from the shelf and took it over to his workbench. 'I'd better start chopping this up. That brontosaurus wants to collect his knickerbockers today.' He grabbed a flint knife and sliced smoothly through the fur. 'James can stitch them together when he gets here! *If* he gets here!'

'Did someone mention my name?' called James from the doorway.

Billy nearly dropped the knife on his foot. 'What *have* you got on?' he gasped.

James was wearing a bright orange and black spotted tunic, and a big purple belt.

'This is my brand new leopard-skin tunic,' said James stretching out his arms and doing a little twirl.

'It looks like someone's been sick on your fur skin!' snorted Billy.

'It's the latest fashion,' said James indignantly. 'No more scratchy mammoth hide for me! Thanks to the dinopants shop, I'm rich. I can spend my precious stones on whatever I want! What do you spend yours on?'

James and Charlie laughed as Billy produced a king-sized bag of liquorice from underneath his workbench.

James headed to his bench, picked up a needle and carefully tried to thread it with some bright yellow yarn. As he did so, a terrifying roar filled the air. James slipped and pricked himself with the needle, yelping in pain.

Charlie put down his tail-hair paintbrush and stood very still. 'What was that?' he asked.

'That was me!' spluttered James. 'I think I might bleed to death!' He held up a tiny scratch for the others to see.

Billy shook his head. 'Not you,' he said, 'the roar. It sounded like —'

Before Billy could finish his sentence the ground began to shake with the sound of pounding footsteps. A second heart-stopping screech filled the air and Charlie's blood ran cold. He looked from James to Billy.

Billy bit his lip nervously. There was only one dinosaur that roared like that.

'T. Rex,' whispered Charlie.

'What's he doing in town?' asked James with a shudder. 'He usually stays out on the mountain.'

They all watched from the door as the people of Sabreton scurried for cover – everyone had heard the T. Rex and they weren't hanging around to find out what he wanted.

A long time ago, the dinosaurs and humans had been at war. Eventually a truce had been agreed between them, and they had lived peacefully side-by-side ever since. But the T. Rex had never been happy with the truce and everyone believed it was only a matter of time before he decided to wage war on the humans again. Charlie had already made the T. Rex very angry with his invention of dinopants, but the T. Rex had eventually been won round and now sported a pair of black leather pants himself. However, Charlie, like everyone else in Sabreton, realised that the T. Rex was still a huge threat. When he ventured down from his mountain everyone panicked.

The boys inched outside. Charlie suddenly felt dinosaur breath on the back of his neck. He turned round slowly and breathed a sigh of relief. It was Steggy, his pet dinosaur! They looked after each other no matter what, and Steggy had rushed to find Charlie as soon as he'd heard the T. Rex's roar.

'The T. Rex wouldn't hurt us, would he?' asked

Charlie, looking at Steggy uncertainly. 'We saved his life once.'

Another ferocious roar filled the air. There, at the end of the dusty high street, stood the mighty figure of the T. Rex. The massive dinosaur towered high above the trees and Charlie watched as he took an angry swipe at a pterodactyl that dared to swoop too close to his head.

Charlie gulped. The T. Rex seemed to recognise him. Suddenly he growled, flared his nostrils and ran straight for the little caveboy. 'On second thoughts, perhaps he *would* hurt us! Hide!'

Everyone ran inside the shop. Charlie slammed the door shut behind him and leaped over the counter and Steggy squeezed in close behind.

Louder and louder, crashing like a thousand drums, the T. Rex's pounding footsteps came towards them. Charlie felt the ground beneath him wobble like an earthquake . . . And then . . . and then . . . everything stopped.

Charlie held his breath. Nothing. He breathed a sigh of relief and popped his head over the top of the counter to take a peek. Just then, the door flew open with a crash, and the T. Rex's huge head filled the entrance. He took one look at Charlie, and roared. Charlie felt his hair quiver as the shop filled with the stench of rotting flesh.

The T. Rex stared at them intently, as if studying a piece of meat on a butcher's slab, and then reached inside the shop, hooked his tail through Charlie's fur skin and dragged him outside. He lifted him high into the air towards his powerful jaws and glistening teeth, and snarled. Charlie closed his eyes, bracing himself for the worst . . .

But then, much to his surprise, he felt himself being lowered down on to the dusty ground. What was going on?

'W-W-What do you want?' stuttered Charlie, his voice trembling with fear and his heart beating hard and fast.

The T. Rex turned and showed Charlie.

'Is that all?' said Charlie with a laugh. 'You terrified me!'

Billy and James, who had been cowering behind the workbenches, gathered in the doorway.

'What does he want, Charlie?' asked Billy.

'He wants us to mend his dinopants!' said Charlie pointing. The T. Rex's dinopants had a large rip in them and he wasn't happy about it at all.

CHAPTER 2

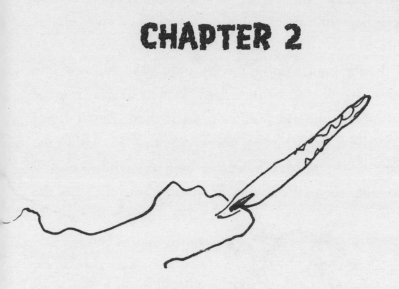

'How did he get a pair of dinopants in the first place?' asked James.

The three boys were back inside the dinopants shop and Charlie was searching the shelves for a roll of thick black yarn.

'I gave him a pair after I saved his life,' said Charlie as he rummaged. 'It was a peace offering.'

'Well, it seems to have worked,' Billy said, smiling. 'He hasn't eaten anyone yet. Look.'

Slowly but surely the townsfolk of Sabreton had emerged from their hiding places and were staring open mouthed at the T. Rex. They had never dared get close to him before. The T. Rex was standing in the town square and trying his best to look noble and majestic while covering his peeping bottom with his tail.

'Right,' said Charlie, 'we've only got a short while before we have to be in school. We haven't got time for him to take the pants off for us to fix them and then put them back on again to check they're OK – it'll take ages. We'll just have to stitch them up while he's still wearing them. Let's not keep him waiting.' Charlie offered James the roll of yarn.

'You want me to do it?' spluttered James in surprise.

'You're the best with a needle and thread.'

'I'm not going any-where near him! You do it!' said James, sticking out his chin defiantly.

'Fine,' said Charlie with a sigh. 'Give me the needle.'

Charlie carefully threaded the needle with black yarn and stepped out into the square. The whole town seemed to have gathered to watch. James and Billy pulled a ladder out from behind the shop and gently propped it against the T. Rex's back. Charlie tried not to shake as he began to climb the rickety steps. Soon he was eye to bum-cheek with the T. Rex.

'Do T. Rexes fart?' asked James, looking up at his friend.

'Let's hope Charlie's down the ladder before we find out,' whispered Billy.

Charlie reached out a quivering hand and pulled the two sides of the rip in the T. Rex's dinopants together. Carefully he began to sew.

After half an hour the dinopants were almost as good as new. As Charlie jumped off the bottom rung of the ladder, the crowd began to clap. Charlie grinned and gave a little bow.

The T. Rex trotted over to Sabreton pond to examine Charlie's handiwork. He gazed at the reflection of his bottom in the water and nodded to himself, before turning to roar his approval at the three boys.

'I think he's saying thank you,' said Charlie, laughing.

The T. Rex smiled, swished his tail proudly and then turned to start the journey back towards his mountain.

As the crowd dispersed, Charlie's dad ran round the corner. He was trying to do up his leopard-skin tie and finish his breakfast at the same time. 'Sorry boys! I overslept!'

'Did you see the T. Rex, Dad?' asked Charlie. 'I stitched up his dinopants!'

'You stitched up his what?' spluttered Charlie's father. 'You'll have to tell me all about it – but later! You boys had better get to school.'

The three boys looked up at the sun. It was already a quarter of the way across the sky.

'We'd better run!' said Charlie.

'Too right!' replied James. 'There's only one thing more terrifying than a T. Rex . . .'

'Mrs Heavystep when she's angry!' they all chorused as they took off towards the school.

'Don't worry about the shop!' called Charlie's dad after them. 'It's in safe hands with me and Steggy!'

Charlie's dad had given up his job as an inventor to help run the shop while the boys were at school. He delivered orders, sent out for fresh stock and looked after all of the precious stones and food that the dinosaurs used to pay for their dinopants. He loved his job.

Steggy helped in the shop too. He was the official dinopants model. There was a painting of him on the front of the dinopants shop and on advertisements that had been drawn on walls all over Sabreton.

Charlie's dad looked at the line of dinosaurs that were waiting to collect their orders and smiled. It was going to be another busy day.

CHAPTER 3

Charlie and his two friends ran up the high street, past the town hall and on towards school. The school was a large stone building on the outskirts of Sabreton. It was surrounded by dusty playing fields and, as they zoomed past a tired old centrosaurus, the goalposts on the football pitch came into view.

'Oh dear,' said James pointing ahead.

Mrs Heavystep, their teacher, was standing by the school entrance tapping her foot. She didn't look very happy.

Charlie flashed her a weak smile as the three boys skidded to a halt.

'Don't tell me!' she fumed. 'Dinopants!'

Charlie nodded and tried to explain. 'I'm sorry, miss, but you know the T. Rex was in town and he needed me to mend his knickers and then we didn't realise the time and we had to —'

'Enough!' barked Mrs Heavystep, pointing to the classroom where the rest of the children were waiting. 'You've wasted plenty of time already this morning. Get in!' Charlie looked around the classroom

for a seat. The class was full of children sitting on big smooth rocks arranged around slate tables. Natalie Honeysuckle stood up and waved in his direction. Charlie tried to ignore her. He had a not-so-secret crush on Natalie and he knew that James and Billy would tease him if he ended up sitting next to her. It was no use though – Natalie was waving so hard Charlie was sure her arm would fly off if he didn't go and sit down soon.

'I saved it for you,' she whispered with a smile as Charlie walked towards his seat.

Billy giggled and winked in his direction. James cooed and pretended to kiss an imaginary girlfriend. Charlie stuck out his tongue and blew a raspberry at his two mocking friends.

'That's enough of that, Charlie Flint!' Mrs Heavystep snapped.

Charlie put his tongue back in and went bright red.

'Now, today we have a very special visitor,' said Mrs Heavystep. 'So please give a big Sabreton School welcome to Barry Relic!'

'Barry who?' asked James, as the class began to clap.

Billy shrugged his shoulders.

A strange old man creaked into the classroom. He had a long silver beard and walked with a stick. His fur skin was grey and shabby – whatever colour it had once been had been washed out long ago. He tottered up to the front of the class and stood next to Mrs Heavystep. It was only when he turned to address the children that Charlie realised he had seen the man before.

'Oh no,' he hissed. 'It's that boring old man from the museum!'

On dull Saturday afternoons, Charlie and his dad would wander up to Sabreton Museum and look at the musty exhibits. It was usually something they did when Charlie's mum had told his dad to do some chores. Barry Relic was the man who ran the museum.

'Mr Relic has come to teach us all how to make sparking flints!' beamed Mrs Heavystep.

The class groaned. Charlie understood why – he couldn't think of a more boring way to spend a morning.

'Really children!' snapped Mrs Heavystep. 'How rude!'

'It's all right,' croaked Barry with a smile. 'I'm used to it! Sparking flints sound dull, don't they?'

One or two of the children nodded.

'Well, let me tell you there is nothing dull about a sparking flint! Imagine being trapped in a cave in the middle of the night. You've got nothing to eat and you're freezing cold. What are you going to do?' Mr Relic swung his walking stick dramatically and pointed at James. 'What are *you* going to do?'

James shrugged his shoulders. 'Eat my fingernails and jog on the spot?'

The class began to laugh. Mrs Heavystep shot James a withering look.

Mr Relic cackled. 'A fine explorer you'd be! No! You'd take out your sparking flint and start up a fire!' With a flourish Mr Relic whipped out his sparking flint and struck it against the school wall. Sparks flashed all around him. 'With this you need never be hungry or cold again! After your club, a sparking flint is the only tool a caveboy – or cavegirl –' Mr Relic gave Natalie a toothless smile, 'will ever need.'

'Brilliant!' gasped James. 'Where do I buy one?'

Mr Relic cackled again. 'You don't *buy* sparking flints! A sparking flint has to be made by the person who's going to use it. It has to fit the owner, see? I made this sparking flint myself when I was about your age. See how it still fits the shape of my hand?'

Mr Relic held it up for the boys and girls to see. 'A true sparking flint is as much a part of your hand as your fingers or thumb and today I'm going to teach you how to make one that will last you for the rest of your life.' He struck his flint against the wall and he was showered in sparks once again.

Outside a strange wheezing noise filled the air.

'Ah good,' said Mr Relic, 'the rocks have arrived. Follow me everyone!'

The children followed Mr Relic out on to the playing field where a large triceratops was standing next to a cart filled with rocks.

'This is Teresa,' said Mr Relic patting the triceratops on her wrinkly grey neck. 'She's nearly as old as me! Now, everybody take a rock and we'll go back inside and get started.'

Excitedly the children grabbed one rock each and headed back to their seats. For the next little while, Mr Relic showed them how to smooth out the rock and then how to chip away at it to get the perfect sparking flint.

'There's no rights or wrongs when it comes to sparking flints,' he explained. 'Every one of you is unique and every one of your sparking flints will be unique too. Just make sure it fits snugly between your thumb and forefinger.'

Charlie took to making sparking flints as if he had been doing it all his life.

'Well done, Charlie,' said Mr Relic as he made his way around the class examining the children's handiwork. 'That looks like a good one. Of course, I wouldn't have expected anything less from a boy with a name like yours. Charlie Flint! It must be in your blood!'

By lunchtime, everyone in the class was the proud owner of a brand new sparking flint. Mr Relic asked the children to form a line down the side of the classroom and one by one they sparked their flints against the wall. While they were waiting their turn, Billy went on and on at Charlie about him being the class swot.

Charlie was just about to bring his flint down on the rock wall when the room was filled with the sound of a trumpet. Standing in the

doorway was the mayor of Sabreton's bodyguard, Boris.

The burly body-guard wore a fur skin adorned with shiny medals and parped importantly on a wooden trumpet. Once his fanfare had finished, the mayor marched proudly into the classroom. He was wearing his ceremonial fur skin, a precious stone dangled from around his neck and he had a moustache that bristled as he scanned the room.

'Leslie Trumpbottom!' exclaimed Mrs Heavystep. 'I haven't had you in my classroom since the day I taught you how to mend a fur skin! You stitched yourself to the curtains, remember?'

Everyone in the class laughed and the mayor blushed.

'Yes, w-well . . .' he stuttered, 'I haven't come here to talk about the old days. I need to see Charlie Flint. Is he here?'

Charlie put up his hand and waved at the mayor.

'I have to talk to you right now, Charlie.'

Mrs Heavystep coughed and glared at the mayor.

'Actually, after school will be fine,' said the mayor, smiling nervously at Mrs Heavystep. 'We don't want to interrupt any more of your lesson, do we? Meet me at Dinopoo Field. There's something I need to show you. We have a problem . . .'

'What sort of problem?' gasped Charlie.

'Later, Charlie!' he said and marched back out of the classroom. Boris saluted and scurried close behind.

'On that note, I think it's time for lunch,' announced Mrs Heavystep. 'So please put your sparking flints in your pockets and give Mr Relic a warm round of applause.'

The children clapped as they filed out into the playground. Mr Relic waved, climbed up on Teresa and trotted back towards his museum.

Charlie tried to concentrate on the game of football he played with Billy and James that lunchtime, but he couldn't stop thinking about what the mayor had said. What problem could he mean and how did he expect Charlie to help?

CHAPTER 4

'Don't do that!' exclaimed Billy as James poked suspiciously at a steaming pile of diplodocus dung with a long stick. 'It's fresh and it hasn't settled yet!'

'Why do you know so much about poo?' asked James. 'Sometimes I wonder why we're friends at all!'

The diplo-dung squelched and wobbled dangerously as the pile towered above them.

'I'm not coming to rescue you if it falls on your head!' warned Charlie.

After school, Billy and James had said that they wanted to go and meet the mayor too. Then Steggy had arrived looking for a game of hide-and-seek. Charlie couldn't say no to any of his friends, so all four of them were now making their way down the track that led to Dinopoo Field.

Charlie shook his head. They'd never get there if they stopped to examine every pile of dinopoo they found along the way. Billy was an expert hunter and had a strange fascination with details, especially dinopoo.

'You can tell a lot about a dinosaur from its poo,' he boasted. 'You can see what it's eaten and everything.'

The pile of diplo-dung wobbled again.

'Leave it!' snapped Charlie, and marched on determinedly with Steggy.

'Fine. There's plenty more where that came from!' huffed Billy as he scurried over to examine another pile.

'Steggy plop-plops!' he gushed as he knelt beside a mucky green heap. 'And look at that lot!' Billy pointed to a mountain of bright blue dinopoo. 'Iguanodon do-do! That's rare!'

As the three boys and Steggy walked down the dusty path, they passed pile after pile of dinopoo.

'Where's it all coming from?' asked James.

'From dinobums!' said Billy sarcastically.

'I know that,' said James, 'but I thought they were supposed to be pooing in Dinopoo Field, not out on the road.'

'He's right,' agreed Charlie. 'Dinopoo Field was given to the dinosaurs to stop this sort of thing.'

Dinopoo Field was a piece of dusty scrubland that lay just outside Sabreton. The dinosaurs visited it whenever they needed to poo. There they could drop their dinopants and poo freely. It had been a great success and now there was no dinopoo in Sabreton. Every dinosaur visited Dinopoo Field at least once a day, sometimes twice depending on what they'd been eating. But why weren't they using it any more?

'What's the problem, Steggy?' asked Charlie.

Steggy pointed his tail towards Dinopoo Field.

'W-What's happened?' stuttered Charlie.

Dinopoo Field was gone – in its place was a dense jungle filled with weird and wonderful plants and trees. Some were yellow, some were blue, some had prickly thorns and towered high above the caveboys.

Ahead of them, a triceratops was trying to barge his

way through the vines and tendrils into the field, but even with his three big horns he couldn't manage it – the plants were just too thick. In the end, he lowered his dinopants and pooed where he stood.

'Gross!' said James sticking out his tongue.

'What else is he supposed to do?' asked Billy. 'Poo in his pants?'

As they watched, a massive diplodocus struggled out of the field. He had four purple flowers on top of his head, which only just  cleared the tops of the trees. He looked up and smiled at the three boys. His teeth were peppered with brightly coloured petals.

Charlie gave the diplodocus a weak wave. 'At least he's still trying to use Dinopoo Field.'

'Yeah,' agreed James, 'but if one of the biggest dinosaurs is finding it difficult, what chance have little ones like Steggy got?'

'My point exactly,' said the mayor, arriving with

Boris. 'You see our problem, Charlie? It was just a dusty old patch of land until the dinosaurs started to poo on it. Over the last few months these plants and trees have sprouted up. It's got completely out of hand!'

'There must be something in the dinopoo that's good for the soil,' mused Billy.

'Indeed,' said the mayor, nodding, 'and now because all the dinopoo is in the same place we get this!' He pointed at the jungle of sharp thorns and brambles. 'Imagine pricking your bottom on one of those every time you needed to do your business!'

Charlie and Billy winced. James rubbed his bottom in sympathy.

'If the dinosaurs can't get into Dinopoo Field to do their . . . their . . .'

'Steggy-plop-plops?' offered Billy.

'Thank you,' said the mayor. 'They just go wherever they can. They're already leaving dinopoo in the road! Soon it will be back on the high street, back by our homes and back on your football pitch too!'

The boys grimaced.

'We could just make the field bigger,' offered Charlie.

'At this rate we'd need a new field every few months. We simply haven't any more clear fields to offer them,' said the mayor. 'The only solution is to close the dinopants shop.'

The three boys and Steggy turned to stare at the mayor open mouthed.

'What?' gasped Charlie. 'Why? It's not my dinopants that are causing this problem, it's the dinopoo!'

'I have no other choice, Charlie,' said the mayor shaking his head sadly. 'If it was just the dinosaurs of Sabreton using Dinopoo Field then there'd still be plenty of room for ...'

'Iguanodon do-do?' suggested Billy.

'Exactly,' nodded the mayor. 'But your dinopants shop has been so successful we've got dinosaurs coming from all over the place to buy dinopants and they all use Dinopoo Field too. We simply can't cope with all that extra dinopoo! We need to stop these dinosaurs coming into town and that means getting rid of the reason why they come — your shop!'

'But . . . but . . . but . . .' said Charlie.

'My decision is final!' said the mayor. 'I'm sorry, boys.' With that, he turned and walked back towards Sabreton with Boris following.

James and Billy looked at Charlie. He was very upset. Steggy nuzzled his cheek gently.

'What are you going to do?' asked Billy.

'I don't know,' said Charlie, shaking his head sadly. 'I just don't know.'

CHAPTER 5

'Well, there's no point standing around here being miserable,' said James clapping his hands. 'We've got a dinopants shop to run.'

'For one evening only,' muttered Charlie sadly.

'Don't be like that,' said Billy. 'It was brilliant while it lasted. We should remember all the good times we've had making the pants. There were your wacky designs, the lovely dinosaurs we met, and who could forget Steggy and all his modelling.'

Steggy smiled and gave the boys a proud bow.

'And I've never seen the town looking so clean,' continued Billy.

'And the smell's gone!' added James.

'And I've been able to afford lots of liquorice!' smiled Billy patting his stomach. He walked over, put a tree-trunk arm around Charlie's shoulder and gave him a friendly squeeze. 'Let's enjoy our last few hours in the dinopants shop while we can.'

Charlie shook his head. He didn't want to sit in his shop knowing that it was going to be closed in the morning. He shrugged Billy away. 'You two go back,' he said sadly, 'and take Steggy with you. I'm going to stay out here for a bit. I want to be on my own – I need some time to think.'

Steggy wandered over and gave Charlie one of his biggest licks. It covered Charlie's whole face in slobber.

Charlie couldn't help but smile as he slopped the goo on to the ground.

'All right,' sighed Charlie, 'you can stay!'

Steggy wagged his tail in delight.

'Do you want to give me a ride? It might help me think of a way to save the shop.'

Steggy smiled and crouched down. Charlie clambered up on to his friend's big green back and held on tight. As they trotted past Dinopoo Field and away from Sabreton, Charlie began to think.

He couldn't let the mayor close the dinopants shop. He just couldn't! Charlie enjoyed being known as the boy who had solved the dinopoo problem. If the shop closed no one would think that any more. He'd be the boy who had tried and failed to solve the dinopoo problem. It would have been better if he hadn't tried in the first place.

But it wasn't just that: people depended on him. His dad and his friends loved working in the shop. It wasn't so bad for Billy and James, but if the shop closed his dad would have to go back to the old job he hated so much. Charlie couldn't let that happen.

It wasn't the dinopants that were the problem, it was the dinopoo. If he could get rid of that then maybe the mayor would change his mind.

We could pile the dinopoo up in one place, thought Charlie, like Dinopoo Field only better. Instead of leaving it on the ground, someone could go along with a shovel and pile it somewhere out of the way.

Charlie shook his head. It would never work. Before long you'd have a hill-sized pile of dinopoo on the outskirts of Sabreton. After a few months it would be the size of a mountain and after a year it would be the biggest mountain in the world – even bigger than T. Rex's mountain.

Charlie imagined a huge mountain of dinopoo towering over Sabreton. A stinky, wobbly mountain with its top lost in the clouds. And what if there was a poo-slide? It didn't bear thinking about. Sabreton

would be smothered in dinopoo. What a way to go!

Charlie shuddered. Dinopoo Mountain was a big no-no.

Above him a pterodactyl swooped majestically in the air before coming to land in one of the tall plants in Dinopoo Field. At least somebody liked the flowers, thought Charlie.

Steggy turned to look at him. Was it time to go home?

'Just a little bit further,' said Charlie, patting Steggy's neck. 'We'll be home before it gets dark, I promise.'

We could try and *use* the dinopoo, thought Charlie as they walked. But what would you use dinopoo for? Maybe you could live in it! Charlie wrinkled his nose at the thought. He imagined people making houses out of dinopoo and stuck out his tongue. Who'd want to live in a dinopoo house? It'd stink! You'd have to build a little village of them somewhere outside Sabreton to make sure nobody complained. Charlie smiled. You could call it Stenchton or Pongyville and fill it with all the people you didn't like! He shook his head – he'd have to think harder if he wanted his shop to stay open.

Charlie and Steggy were nearing the gentle slopes of the hills. It was time to turn back towards Sabreton before it got too late, but the ride had given Charlie bum-ache – he needed a bit of a break before he began the journey home.

'Let me down, Steggy!' he called.

Steggy stopped and crouched so that Charlie could clamber off his back. Charlie landed in the soft grass that grew at the foot of the hills.

Charlie looked up at Steggy. 'Why can't you do what we do?' he asked.

Steggy looked confused.

When humans needed to poo they dug holes in the ground and covered it up after they'd finished. But

their poos were small so you only needed a little hole. But some dinosaur poos were massive so you'd be digging for hours before you had a hole big enough to poo into and by then it would be too late!

Perhaps someone could dig the holes for them, thought Charlie. He shook his head. Dinosaurs pooed so much you'd need a whole army of people working day and night just to keep up. And if you wanted to bury all the dinopoo you'd have to keep finding new places to dig the holes. Before long you'd be walking miles just to find a fresh place to dig.

What he needed was something that could get rid of the dinopoo altogether. But what would do that? He

lay down on the soft grass and Steggy lay near him. The noise of rushing water filled his ears – there was a river beneath him, under the ground.

Charlie remembered something Mrs Heavystep had told them in class a couple of weeks before. She had been talking about water and its uses and had said that water was one of the most powerful things known to man – that it might look soft and harmless but it could be strong enough to wash away even the largest rock. The class hadn't believed her at first but then she'd told them all about the underground river. It had formed

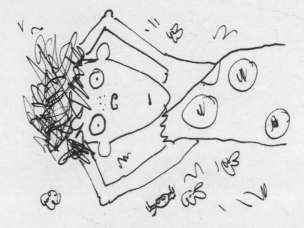

deep under the earth by rubbing away at the rock over thousands and thousands of years.

It was then that an idea popped into Charlie's head. He sat up and looked at the ground. If he could hear the river then it couldn't be very far below him, and if water could wash away rock then surely it could wash away dinopoo too. He picked up a sharp stone and began to scrape at the earth. Before long he had dug a little hole.

After a few more minutes of digging, Charlie felt the ground at the bottom of the hole crumble. Cold air rushed out with a whistle. When Charlie put his ear to the hole he could hear the sound of rushing water, louder than ever. He was right over the underground river! He peered inside and could see the early evening sunlight reflected on the water a few metres below.

'It *will* work!' said Charlie punching the air. 'It really will work!'

Deep underground a creature stirred. It sniffed the air and hissed. Something had woken it. A noise. A scraping, scratching noise from somewhere above. A thin slither of sunlight shone through the ceiling and on to the river.

The creature squeezed its eyes shut. It couldn't stand bright light – it liked nothing but beautiful darkness. The creature spat some green gloop past two razor-sharp fangs and stretched out a forked tongue. It didn't like being woken up. It didn't like being woken up at all.

CHAPTER 6

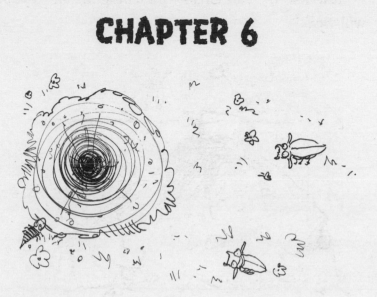

'I call it the dinoloo,' said Charlie proudly.

'I call it a hole,' muttered James, staring at the hole over the underground river the following morning.

Charlie tutted. 'You have to use your imagination.'

Charlie had persuaded Billy and James to come out to the underground river before school so that he could explain his big idea to them.

'Don't you see?' said Charlie. He was getting frustrated now. 'It's the answer to our prayers. It'll get rid of dinopoo for ever.'

'How —?' began Billy, but he was interrupted by the sound of footsteps. It was the mayor walking briskly towards them. His moustache bristled and his ceremonial stone swung from side to side as he marched. Boris was jogging close behind.

'You invited the mayor!' said James, slapping his forehead.

'Of course!' Charlie winked.

'Here we go again,' mumbled Billy, shaking his head slowly.

'Now, Charlie,' said the mayor, 'your message said that you had something to show me. It had better be important. It's very early in the morning, you know.'

'Tell me about it,' yawned Billy quietly.

Charlie cleared his throat and addressed the mayor. 'Mr Mayor, I believe I have the answer to the dinopoo problem. My new invention will ensure that my dinopants shop can stay open and that we need never worry about the rather stinky problem of dinopoo again!'

The mayor arched an eyebrow.

'Mr Mayor, I give you the dinoloo!'

Charlie stepped to one side and gestured grandly to the ground.

The mayor peered down. 'Where is it, Charlie?' he asked.

'It's right there,' said Charlie, pointing at the hole.

'That's just a hole,' muttered the mayor.

'Exactly what I said,' said James, nodding.

The mayor looked at Charlie. The corner of his mouth began to twitch. 'Are you having a laugh?'

'It's no joke, Mr Mayor! Let me explain. What do we do when we want to get rid of our dirt?'

James, Billy and the mayor looked at each other. There was an embarrassed silence.

'We bury it!' said

55

Charlie excitedly. 'Only dinosaurs can't do that, can they? They don't have fingers and the holes they'd have to dig would be massive. So what can we do instead?'

The mayor shrugged his shoulders.

'We can dig the hole for them.'

The mayor thought for a moment. 'But won't that fill up very quickly?'

'Not if we dig the hole over the underground river.' Charlie pointed at the hole.

Billy began to smile. Charlie was right – if you built the hole over an underground river then the poo would float away and the hole would never fill up. No one would see it, no one would smell it – it was perfect!

'Brilliant!' gushed Billy.

'I see!' spluttered the mayor. 'The dinopoo floats away under the ground!'

'Exactly,' smiled Charlie. 'And just to prove it works I've brought Steggy along to demonstrate.'

Steggy gulped. He hadn't been told about this.

Charlie began to make the hole a little bigger.

'Come on, Steggy!' he called. 'Let's show them how it works.'

Steggy wandered nervously towards the hole and pulled down his dinopants.

'Go on, Steggy,' encouraged James with a wink. 'Steggy-plop-plop!'

Steggy pulled his dinopants back up and began to blush.

'What's the matter?' asked the mayor, looking at Charlie. 'Doesn't he need to go?'

'I think he's a little bit embarrassed,' said Charlie. 'Is that it, Steggy?'

Steggy nodded his head.

'I see his point,' said Billy. 'How would you like to go with everyone watching you?'

'I'm sorry, Steggy,' said Charlie. 'I should have thought of that.'

Steggy gave Charlie a big sloppy lick just to show there were no hard feelings.

'Well, Charlie,' said the mayor shaking his head, 'it's a very good idea, but if the dinosaurs are too embarrassed to use a dinoloo then I'm afraid it doesn't solve our problem, does it? Your dinopants shop will still have to close.'

'What if we build something around the dinoloo so that the dinosaurs can poo in privacy?' said Charlie.

'Like a fence?' James offered.

'Exactly!' agreed Charlie as he picked up a stick and drew in the dust. 'Something like this.'

The mayor looked at the sketch. Charlie had drawn a little hut with a dinosaur sitting inside it.

'Would that do the trick, Steggy?' he asked.

Steggy nodded and smiled.

'Then that settles it,' said the mayor. 'Let's give it a go!'

Charlie and James began to cheer, but Billy was still deep in thought.

'Hang on!' he said waving his arms in the air and cutting the celebrations short. He pointed at Charlie's picture. 'That dinoloo is tiny. Steggy might be able to use it but a diplodocus would never get inside. Some dinobums are bigger than others. If you make the hole too big, then the little dinosaurs will fall straight through and get carried away to a very stinky end. And if you make the holes too small, then the big dinosaurs won't be able to get their bums over them at all!'

'He's right, Charlie,' said the mayor. 'We'd never get a dinoloo to fit every dinosaur bottom.'

'Then we build a few!' said Charlie thinking on his feet once more. 'We build three huts in a row right here!' Charlie began drawing again. 'They each have a different-sized hole inside. One is for dinosaurs with big bums, one is for dinosaurs with small bums and one is for dinosaurs whose bum is somewhere in-between. They just pick the right dinoloo for them!'

The mayor bristled his moustache. 'And who would build these dinoloos?' he asked.

'Us,' Charlie said with a smile.

'What!' spluttered James.

'We'll build them!' agreed Billy.

'Speak for yourself!' muttered James.

'If it means saving Charlie's dinopants shop we'll work day and night if we have to.'

'Day and night,' gasped James. 'Have you gone mad?'

'Please, James,' said Charlie running over to speak to his friend. 'If you help me, I promise I'll buy you the most expensive fur skin Mrs Glam has in her shop.'

James narrowed his eyes and thought for a moment. 'The one made out of pterodactyl skin?'

'If you want!'

James thought again.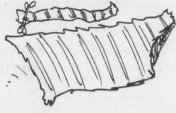
'With a matching belt?'

'Anything.'

James smiled and offered Charlie his hand. 'It's a deal!'

Charlie and James shook on it.

The mayor looked at the three friends and smiled. 'All right, build your dinoloos. If they work, your dinopants shop can stay open for as long as you like.'

'Come on, guys!' said Charlie, clapping his hands and turning to walk with the mayor back towards Sabreton. 'There's no time to waste – we've got work to do!'

CHAPTER 7

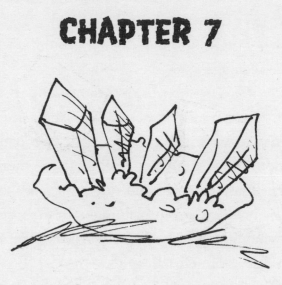

For the next two weeks, Charlie and his friends worked as hard as they could to build three brand new dinoloos on the outskirts of Sabreton. Every morning before school and every afternoon afterwards they would head out to the foothills and work until it got too dark to see.

Charlie's dad had agreed to put in extra hours at the dinopants shop and he had used some precious stones to buy large planks of wood from Mr Blade the lumberjack. Steggy helped too — he carried all of the heavy planks from Sabreton to the hillside and used his strength to hold them in place while the boys cut, slotted and tied them together with vine ropes.

The boys started by digging three holes all the way down to the underground river tunnel and then built the huts over the top. With a bit of luck, the dinopoo would fall straight through the holes, into the river and never be seen again.

When the dinoloos were finished, three roofless wooden huts stood in a row in the shade of the lush green hills. As well as the dinoloos, the boys had built a little booth for an attendant to sit in. It was their job to keep the dinoloos clean and tidy and make sure that the dinosaurs used the right dinoloo for their bum size.

'So who's going to be the attendant?' asked Billy.

'You'll see,' said Charlie with a wink.

Charlie's dad popped his head out of the booth. The

boys began to laugh. He was wearing a big pointy hat made out of blue dyed fur. He also had a wooden badge with a picture of a dinoloo hut stuck to his chest.

'I think he makes a very good dinoloo attendant,' said Charlie. 'I made the uniform myself. And Mum says she'll look after the shop while he's here. Now, are we all ready? We don't want to keep our public waiting!'

Charlie nodded at the small crowd of people that had gathered around them. They had come all the way to the hillside to witness the grand opening of the dinoloos. There was a strip of hide stretched across the door of the largest one and Billy was holding a pair of scissor flints. The air was filled with the tooting of a wooden trumpet and the mayor and Boris appeared over the brow of the hill. The assembled townsfolk gave them a polite round of applause and then the mayor began to speak.

'As you know,' he said in his poshest and most mayor-like voice, 'we are here today to open Sabreton's first ever dinoloos. We hope they will prove to be a permanent solution to our dinopoo problem. Young Charlie Flint and his two friends . . .'

Steggy coughed and fixed the mayor with a fierce glare.

The mayor quickly corrected himself. ' . . . Sorry, *three* friends, have done an excellent job. And it is my great pleasure to declare Sabreton Dinoloos open!'

Billy handed the mayor his scissor flints and with a big grin and a trumpet parp from Boris, the mayor cut the hide.

Once the mayor had left, Steggy was given the honour of being the first dinosaur ever to use a dinoloo. He blew a few kisses to the crowd before marching through the small-sized door to produce one of his steggy-plop-plops.

The crowd heard it splosh into the underground river and cheered. Steggy came back out and gave the crowd a little bow.

'Look at that!' said Charlie shaking his head. 'He thinks he's famous! First he was a dinopants model and now this!'

'You've created a monster,' agreed Billy.

Later that day, the fanged creature stirred once more in its underground home. It sniffed the air with two oily nostrils and hissed. There had been a lot of noise recently and now there was an even worse smell! The creature stretched out its endless pairs of legs and went to investigate. As it clicked down the tunnel it felt the walls with its pincers, finding its way through the darkness. Its fangs dripped with slime.

The creature arrived at the river and its long body swished to a halt. The smell was everywhere. The river rushed into a large shallow pool before flowing on through a narrow, thin tunnel.

Its dull green eyes flashed with anger as it took in the scene. There was nasty stuff in the pool. It was bobbing and floating on the surface, filling the air with a terrible stench. There was so much of it! As it watched, a big pile of diplo-dung splashed into the pool and floated towards the narrow tunnel. The tunnel opening was getting clogged with dinopoo and so the water wasn't flowing as freely as it had been. Before long the water would have nowhere to go and the whole pool would be filled with dinopoo. The creature hissed, rose up on its back legs and thrashed the air in disgust. It had to tell the king. Something had to be done.

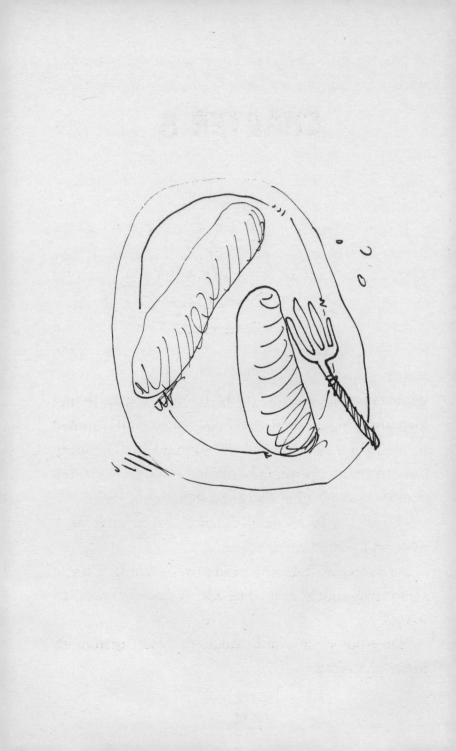

CHAPTER 8

The following morning, Charlie was sitting in the kitchen eating a celebration breakfast of sabre-toothed tiger sausages and a pterodactyl-egg omlette. The room was filled with the sound of sizzling as his mum speared another sausage on a sharpened stick over the fire.

'Thanks, Mum,' said Charlie, cramming in a mouthful. 'These are delicious.'

At the same time, his mum was making Charlie some mammoth-meat vine-leaf wraps to take to school.

'Do you want radish sauce on your mammoth meat?' she asked.

Charlie stuck out his tongue and pretended to be sick. 'I'll take that as a no!' she laughed.

Charlie swigged back his milk and reached for another sausage. 'Will Dad want any of these?' he asked gesturing to the rapidly emptying plate.

'He's already left for the dinoloos,' said his mum, wrapping the vine leaves in a piece of scraped hide. 'I think he likes his new attendant's job even more than his old one at the shop.'

Just at that moment, the cave door burst open with a crash and Charlie's dad appeared. His face was red from running and his uniform was covered in dust. He steadied himself in the doorway and tried to catch his breath.

Charlie looked up in surprise. 'What's the matter, Dad?'

Charlie's dad waved an arm at him. He was panting too much to speak.

'George?' said Charlie's mum. 'What's happened?'

'Dinoloo . . .' he gasped, 'broken . . . monster . . .'

'George,' said Charlie's mum, offering her husband a beaker of water, 'you're not making any sense!'

Charlie's dad gulped down the water, before rushing over, grabbing Charlie by the shoulders and fixing him with a steady stare. Then he opened his mouth and began to speak again. He was so panicked it came out as garbled nonsense.

'It'sthedinoloosomethingterriblehashappened! Monster!'

'Slow down, Dad!' said Charlie. 'I don't understand!'

Charlie's dad took a deep breath and tried again. 'It's the dinoloos, Charlie. Something terrible has happened. I think it's a monster! No time to explain. Come on!'

He grabbed his son by the arm and pulled him out of the cave. Before Charlie had time to think, his dad had yanked him through the garden

gate and out on to the high street.

'Where are you taking me?' panted Charlie as they ran.

'To the dinoloos! You have to see for yourself!'

Charlie's mind began to race. What had happened to his dinoloos? They'd only been open for one day. Surely they couldn't be broken already? And what was all this nonsense about a monster?

'In a hurry, Charlie?' called Billy as Charlie and his dad pelted past him and James, who were on their way to school.

Charlie shouted as he whizzed past, 'There's trouble at the dinoloos! Follow me!'

As they all neared the dinoloos, it was obvious that something wasn't right. Two of the dinoloos looked fine, but all that remained of the largest one was a pile of splintered logs.

'What happened?' gasped Charlie as he took in the scene.

'All our hard work,' moaned Billy, 'gone!'

'That's what I was trying to tell you,' spluttered Charlie's dad. 'Something's destroyed one of your dinoloos.'

'What would be strong enough to do that?' asked Charlie.

'A T. Rex?' suggested James.

'A diplodocus?' offered Billy.

'A monster,' said Charlie's dad, his eyes growing wide.

'There's no such thing as monsters!' Charlie replied.

'Then how do you explain these?' asked his dad, pointing to the ground near the wrecked dinoloo, which was covered with the strangest tracks any of the boys had ever seen.

'There isn't an animal alive that would make tracks like that,' said Billy slowly.

Charlie bent down to examine the tracks. There were no footprints or claw marks, just hundreds of little scratches. It was as if someone had pricked the ground with the end of a stick over and over again.

'What creature did this?' whispered Charlie, sticking his finger into one of the hundreds of holes.

'Something big enough and angry enough to knock down your dinoloo,' said James.

'And something that leaves stuff like this behind it.' Charlie's dad stuck his hand into a big pile of bright green gloop and slopped it on to the ground.

A shiver went down Charlie's spine. He

had never seen anything like it in his life. The gloop was everywhere.

'A monster,' Charlie's dad said.

'A monster,' Charlie agreed, quietly. 'We have to tell the mayor. If there's a monster on the loose, then Sabreton's in grave danger.'

CHAPTER 9

It didn't take long for Charlie's dad and the boys to reach the town hall. They barged straight into the mayor's office and told him all about the destroyed dinoloo and the strange tracks they had found. The mayor put down his cup of nettle tea and gulped.

'You'd better show me,' he said, pulling on his ceremonial stone and calling for Boris to join them.

Out at the dinoloos, the mayor examined the tracks. 'Oh dear,' muttered the mayor to himself. 'Oh dear, oh dear, oh dear.' The mayor's face had gone ash white. He looked very worried indeed. 'I've seen these tracks before,' he said. He stuck his finger into

the disgusting green gloop, deep in thought.

'Where?' demanded Charlie. 'Tell me!'

'First things first,' said the mayor asserting his authority. 'Mr Flint, you need to stay here and look after the other two dinoloos – they look like they'll be in great demand.' He pointed to the brow of the hill where the first few dinosaurs were coming into view. They were heading for the dinoloos.

Charlie's dad began to protest but the mayor dismissed him with a wave. 'Don't worry, Mr Flint, Charlie and his friends will be quite safe with me.'

Next the mayor turned to Boris. 'Go and tell Mrs Heavystep that these boys are going to be late for school. I have something I need to show them that simply can't wait. Follow me.'

★ ★ ★

'Sabreton Museum!' spluttered James looking up at the musty cave building where the mayor had led them. 'What are we doing here?'

'You'll see,' said the mayor as the three boys followed him into the gloomy foyer.

The museum was a large open cave filled with all kinds of objects. A pile of animal skulls were heaped on a slate table and the largest mammoth skin Charlie had ever seen covered one of the walls. Flints of differing sizes were on display in a far corner and a large tusk was balanced on a plinth near the entrance. Charlie went over to have a look.

'Beautiful, isn't she?'

Charlie nearly jumped out of his skin. Barry Relic had appeared behind him.

'Are you here for the tour?' he asked, flashing Charlie a toothless grin.

Charlie didn't know what to say. Before he could speak, Billy, James and the mayor marched over.

'Barry!' said the mayor. 'Thank goodness you're here!'

'Where else would I be? Only time I leave this place is to teach the children about sparking flints.' Barry turned to Charlie. 'How's yours working by the way? Had a chance to try it out yet?'

'Not yet,' said Charlie reaching into his pocket to finger the sharp stone.

Barry turned back to the mayor. 'If I'd known you were coming, your honour, I'd have got the place ready for you. Won't be a minute!'

'No, Barry,' began the mayor, 'there's really no need ...'

But it was too late – Barry had already disappeared into the darkness. He returned a moment later carrying a torch made out of grass and leaves. He lit it with his sparking flint and wandered around the museum

 lighting the other torches that hung from the walls.

As the museum gradually flickered to life, Charlie and his friends got to see more of the exhibits. There were stuffed animals, basins filled with bubbling liquids, a clay model of an early cave village and a display of different coloured mushrooms.

'Right,' said Barry, returning to the group and starting up his patter. 'Welcome to Sabreton Museum, home of the famous woolly mammoth of Prickly Forest.' Barry gestured proudly to the mammoth skin hanging from the wall.

The mayor rolled his eyes and tried to stop him, but it was no use.

'We have many weird and wonderful exhibits here in Sabreton Museum, be it the world's oldest rock, John Hefty's prize-winning chucking spear or the largest pterodactyl egg ever found outside Tuskville. There's something for everyone at Sabreton Museum! And once you've finished your tour, don't forget to visit our souvenir shop.'

Barry smiled and pointed to a flat-topped rock by the door. On the table was a pile of rubbish souvenirs. There was some mouldy old liquorice, some rock paintings that looked like they'd been done by a baby, and some semi-precious stone marbles.

'So where do you want to begin?' asked Barry. 'Stalagmite Corner or the World of Fleas?'

The mayor shook his head. 'Neither. We're here to see the special exhibit.'

'All my exhibits are special,' said Barry with a gummy smile.

'No,' said the mayor fixing Barry with a fierce stare. 'The *really* special exhibit.'

The colour drained from Barry's face as he realised

what the mayor was saying. He looked at the three young caveboys and gulped. 'Really, Mr Mayor? Are you sure?'

'Positive,' said the mayor as he raised himself up to his full height, which wasn't very high at all, and tried to look

Barry straight in the eye.

Barry nodded and walked towards an opening in a dark corner of the cave which Charlie hadn't noticed before. He held his torch high so that the boys and the mayor could follow. 'Watch your step!' he called. 'Not many people come down here. Not many people even know down here exists.'

As the boys followed Barry along a corridor, they passed tatty old exhibits and broken rocks. This was clearly a part of the museum visitors didn't usually see.

Barry stopped next to an old wooden door set into the cave wall and pushed it open with a creak. 'This,' he said, 'is the secret room of Sabreton Museum.'

'When I said I'd seen those strange tracks before,' began the mayor, 'I wasn't lying. I had seen them. I'd seen them here.'

The mayor pointed and Barry lowered his torch. On the floor was a piece of hardened clay. It had obviously been dug out of the ground many years before. Charlie bent down to have a closer look and gasped in surprise – the clay was covered in the same pin-prick tracks they had seen at the dinoloos.

'Why haven't you told anyone about this?' asked Charlie.

'What would I tell them?' said the mayor. 'That we have strange tracks in the Museum of Sabreton that no one can explain? Imagine the panic that would cause! Some things are best kept secret, Charlie. Besides, that's not all. Show them, Barry.'

Barry waved his torch into the darkness and illuminated an old cave painting. Charlie peered closer. It was a picture of a millipede, only it wasn't an ordinary millipede – it was massive and it looked like it was about to eat a man.

'This millipede looks huge!' gasped Charlie. 'The painter must have got it wrong.'

The mayor shook his head. 'We don't think so. We can't be sure, but we think this giant millipede made those tracks.'

'What do you mean, you can't be sure?' spluttered James.

'These paintings and tracks are very old, boys,' said the mayor. 'Only the mayor of Sabreton and the curator of the museum know they exist. The mayor before me told me about them when I took over his job, and his predecessor did the same for him, and so on and so on. Until today, Barry and I thought there was nothing to worry about – no one had seen a peep of the giant millipede. We thought it must have died out long before any of us were born.'

'Only it hasn't,' said Charlie, tracing the cave painting with a finger.

'No,' said the mayor, 'obviously it hasn't. For some reason this monster millipede is back, and looking at what it did to your dinoloo, it's not happy. But until we find out more about it and where it came from, you mustn't tell anyone about this.'

The three boys nodded.

'Now, you'd best get to school. There's only one thing more terrifying than a mysterious dinoloo-destroying millipede . . .'

'Mrs Heavystep when she's angry!' chorused the three boys.

* * *

'So do you believe the mayor, Charlie?' asked James as they walked to school. 'Is there really a giant millipede attacking our dinoloos?'

'I don't know,' said Charlie firmly, 'but I'm going to find out. I'm going to camp out by the dinoloos and see if it comes back!'

James stopped and looked at Charlie. He bit his lip. 'But the mayor said —'

'I know what the mayor said,' snapped Charlie, 'but Sabreton's in danger. What if the millipede comes back and decides to attack the town this time? Then we'd all be in trouble! We need to find out where it's come from and why it's doing what it's doing before it's too late.'

'Then count us in,' said Billy quietly.

'What!' spluttered James.

'We want to help.'

Charlie smiled. 'Meet me at the dinoloos at sunset. We'll all tell our mums we're staying at each others' houses. With a bit of luck they won't check up and we'll have the whole night to find this monster.'

Billy nodded.

'Hang on!' gasped James. 'I didn't agree to any of this.'

But it was too late – Billy and Charlie were already on their way.

'Fine!' called James after them. 'I'll come. But if we all get eaten alive by a millipede my mum's going to kill you!'

★ ★ ★

The creatures met in their cavern far beneath the ground. The smell was worse than ever and the stuff was still coming. They had destroyed the humans' construction but they hadn't got the message. They were going to have to go back, and this time they were going to make the message very clear indeed.

CHAPTER 10

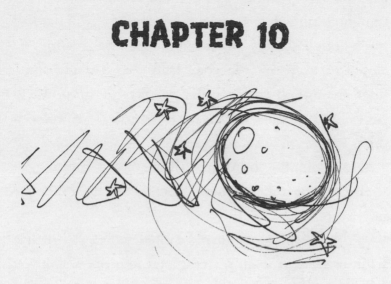

'Can I have a bite?' asked James, eyeing Billy's vine leaf wrap greedily.

'No!' snapped Billy. 'You knew we were coming camping – you should have packed your own.'

'Have some of mine,' said Charlie, offering James a handful of berries.

'Thanks!' James took the berries and fixed Billy with a sulky stare. 'It's at times like this that you know who your true friends are!'

The three boys were sitting in a tent by the dinoloos listening for the millipede. The sun had gone down some time before and a large full moon filled the sky.

Charlie had managed to sneak the tent out of his parents' cave without being seen. It was made from stretched animal hide over a timber frame and had three bone fasteners down one side so that it could be closed to keep out the cold. Billy had brought some thick mammoth-hair fleeces to cover the ground and James had brought three heavy winter fur skins to keep them warm while they waited.

'How long do you think it'll be?' asked Billy.

'I don't know,' admitted Charlie. 'The millipede might not come at all.'

'That would be brilliant,' smiled James. 'I can live without seeing a giant man-eating millipede, thank you very much.'

Charlie pulled open the tent flap and peeked outside. He could see the dark silhouette of the dinoloos and the outline of the hills behind. The campfire they had enjoyed earlier on was dying down and the embers glowed faintly in the darkness.

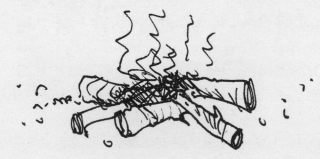

'Do you see anything?' asked Billy.

'Nothing yet,' said Charlie pulling his head back inside and tying the bone fasteners.

'I know!' said James excitedly. 'Let's tell some stories.'

Charlie and Billy groaned. James was always telling stories. They were usually very long and they were always very boring and about himself and the fantastic things he reckoned he'd done.

'Let's not,' said Billy. 'We should get some sleep. We want to be full of energy for when the millipede comes.'

'Just the one!' pleaded James. 'You'll like it! It's scary!'

'I suppose one story won't do any harm,' said Charlie leaning back on the mammoth fleece. 'Besides, if it's as boring as they usually are it might help us sleep!'

James leaned over and punched Charlie on the arm.

'Just for that you're getting the extended version! This story begins on a clear summer evening in a tent not unlike this one. It is the tale of three caveboys who went camping and were never seen again!'

'I might have guessed,' groaned Billy.

'Shush!' said James. 'I'm just getting to the good bit. The three caveboys were fearless monster hunters. There was Casper who was brave and clever, Jason who was good-looking and fashionable, and Brian who was fat and smelled of rotten eggs.'

'Oi!' shouted Billy, playfully.

'One dark night, they were out hunting the most fearsome creature of them all – the giant millipede!'

Suddenly Charlie sat up. He thought he'd heard something outside. 'Shh!' he hissed at James.

'I haven't finished yet!'

'Shh!' hissed Charlie again, pointing to the entrance.

The three boys listened.

Somewhere close by, a twig snapped.

James gulped.

'There's something out there,' whispered Billy.

Charlie put a finger to his lips. The thing outside moved again. It was getting closer. Charlie's heart began to thump. The thing was just outside the tent. He could hear it breathing. Then, there was more rustling. The millipede was moving to the front flap. Charlie looked at his friends – their eyes were wide with terror. Suddenly, one of the bone fasteners popped open.

'It's coming in!' said Billy, now clutching his club.

The three boys squeezed close together and held their breath. The second fastener popped open. The millipede was nearly upon them! The third fastener opened. Charlie closed his eyes. This was it. The tent flaps were ripped apart.

'I knew you were in here!'

Charlie recognised the voice and opened his eyes.

'Wait until I get you home! Your mother's been worried sick! And as for you two . . .' Charlie's dad pointed at Billy and James. 'Don't think your parents won't be told! You'll be grounded for fifteen moons at least!'

Charlie breathed a sigh of relief. His dad may be angry but at least he wasn't a man-eating millipede.

'Camping! With a monster on the loose! I can hardly believe the stupidity of it! I thought you were a smart boy, Charlie, but obviously I was wrong!' Charlie's dad crawled halfway into the tent to shout at the boys some more. 'Honestly! If you want to sneak out somewhere in the middle of the night and you don't want to be found, don't light a campfire! We could see the flames from Sabreton. If there was a monster out here it would have seen them too and —'

He stopped mid-sentence and his eyes grew wide.

'Dad? What is it?'

Charlie's dad suddenly screamed and he was dragged backwards out of the tent. He clawed at the mammoth fleece, trying to grab hold of something. Charlie stretched out his hand but it was too late.

'Dad!' screamed Charlie as his father disappeared.

Charlie, Billy and James watched in horror as the shadow of a long spindly leg prodded and poked at the stretched animal skin above them. Suddenly a razor sharp pincer pierced the roof of the tent and the boys dived out of the way. The pincer seemed to be feeling briefly for anything else that might be lurking inside the tent before disappearing as quickly as it had arrived.

In an instant, the world outside the tent erupted into a cacophony of bangs and crashes. It was like being in the middle of a tornado. Then the sound of splintering wood filled the air.

'It's got my dad!' hissed Charlie, suddenly coming to his senses and scrambling for the tent flap. He couldn't let the millipede take him.

He pulled open a corner of the flap and peered into the darkness. Between the light from the moon and the glow of the embers, Charlie could just about make out not one, but *four* giant millipedes attacking the dinoloos! The cave painting didn't do them justice. They were twice the height of a human, had hundreds and hundreds of legs, and they had two huge curved fangs sticking out from underneath a mouth that was filled with grinding teeth. Their eyes glowed green in the dark and as they smashed the dinoloos with their crab-like pincers, they left a trail of green slime over everything they touched. A fifth millipede stood a little way off, apparently clicking instructions from its strange black mouth. It was even taller than the others and wore a crown of leaves on its head. In its pincer it held the writhing figure of Charlie's father. He was pounding on the pincer with his fists but it made no

difference — the giant millipede wasn't letting go.

'Dad!' screamed Charlie, jumping up. 'I'm coming!'

Billy placed a meaty hand on Charlie's shoulder and pulled him back to the ground. 'No!' he hissed fiercely. 'There's nothing you can do!'

'Dad!' screamed Charlie as Billy held him on the ground. 'Let me go, Billy!'

Charlie bit and scratched at the big boy's arm but still Billy wouldn't release him.

'Billy's right,' said James quietly. 'There's nothing you can do. How is getting yourself caught going to help?'

Charlie struggled and tugged, but it was no use — Billy was too strong. He slumped to the ground, defeated.

The three boys could only watch as the giant millipedes finished breaking the dinoloos. Then the largest of the five clicked some more instructions and

they turned and dived down the biggest dinoloo hole.

'They must live down there!' gasped James.

The last millipede looked at the battered dinoloos and nodded to himself. With Charlie's father still clutched in its pincer, it turned and slithered down the hole itself, and Charlie saw his father's terrified eyes in the moonlight as he disappeared.

CHAPTER 11

Charlie clambered out of the tent and ran towards the hole. He scrambled over the splintered remains of the dinoloos and looked down into the darkness. There was no sign of his dad or the millipedes.

'They've gone,' he said quietly. A tear rolled down his cheek.

'I'm sorry, Charlie,' said Billy.

Charlie turned and fixed his friend with a fierce stare. He knew Billy had been right to hold him back, but he was still angry.

He walked over to the glowing embers of the campfire.

'There was nothing you could have done,' said James softly.

'I shouldn't have invented the dinoloos in the first place,' said Charlie, kicking the ground. 'It was me that let these . . . these . . . things out! If I hadn't dug the dinoloos then they'd still be trapped underground and my dad would still be sitting at home with his feet up! It's all my fault!'

'We should go and tell someone what's happened,' said James quietly. 'Maybe the mayor will know what to do.'

'*I* know what to do,' said Charlie looking at the embers. He turned and scrambled into the tent and

returned with his club. 'Time to go after them.'

'What!' gasped James.

'My dad was still alive when he disappeared into that hole. If we're quick we might be able to rescue him before they . . .' He couldn't bring himself to finish the sentence.

Billy looked at Charlie and nodded. 'If it was my dad that had been taken I'd want to do the same. I'm coming with you.'

'You don't have to,' said Charlie quietly as he bent

down to pick up a glowing branch from the campfire. 'Neither of you do. I'll understand if you want to go back to Sabreton.'

'No,' said Billy firmly. 'You might have managed to tame a T. Rex on your own but you can't take on five giant millipedes!'

'Then I'm coming too,' blurted James.

Billy looked at his friend in surprise. 'I didn't think you were that brave.'

'I'm not,' said James with a worried smile. 'But I'm not staying up here on my own. What if they come back while you're gone?'

Charlie smiled and waved the glowing branch above his head. 'Come on then!' he called. 'There's no time to waste.'

Charlie marched towards the biggest of the three dinoloo holes. He bent down and cleared some logs out of the way. Everything was covered in thick gooey millipede slime. He thrust the branch into the hole. Below him he could see the rippling surface of the river. It didn't look too deep. Charlie picked up one of the vine ropes that the boys had used to create the dinoloos and attached it securely to a tree trunk.

'This should do the trick,' he said as he lowered the rope into the hole. 'I'll go first.'

He handed the fire branch to James and carefully clambered into the hole, shinning down the rope like a monkey.

As he lowered himself into the water, Charlie gasped at its iciness. In shock, he let go of the rope and felt himself tumble into the river. The current was stronger than it looked and Charlie found himself quickly being dragged along beneath the water. His hands scratched the rocky riverbed as he tried to pull himself upright. He gasped for air and breathed in a lungful of freezing water. When his head finally came above the surface, he spluttered as he tried to wedge one foot against a rock to fight the fierce current. Eventually he was standing upright and he struggled towards the side where the river seemed to flow a little slower.

'Are you all right?' called Billy, his booming voice bouncing off the tunnel walls.

Charlie spat out some water and looked up. He could just see his friend's anxious face framed in the dinoloo opening, the moon glowing behind him. Charlie coughed and waved. He was practically frozen to death but nothing was broken.

'I'm fine!' he lied. 'Your turn! Be careful!'

Billy shimmied down the rope and landed in the water with a splash. For Charlie the water was waist deep, but for Billy it only came up to his knees.

James followed, holding the fire branch between his teeth.

'It's f-f-freezing!' said James as he stood shivering in the icy water.

'Then we'd best keep moving,' said Charlie. 'We don't want to be down here any longer than we have to be.'

His two friends nodded in agreement and they began to wade downriver, steadying themselves against the wall as they walked.

The light from the glowing branch wasn't very strong, but it gave the three boys some comfort and warmth as they headed into the darkness. Stalactites hung from the ceiling like giant fangs and icy water dripped on to the boys' heads. Shadows writhed around them and every now and then one of the boys put their hands into a pool of sticky green gloop that had obviously been left on the walls by one of the millipedes.

'At least it shows we're going the right way,' smiled Charlie nervously.

The noise of the river rumbled all around like thunder. As they walked, the river got deeper and stronger until even Billy was having difficulty remaining upright. Then the three boys turned a corner and Charlie stopped. There was another tunnel up ahead, leading away from the river and into the rock.

'Which way now?' shouted Billy over the noise.

Charlie shrugged his shoulders. Should they keep following the river or head up the new tunnel? The millipedes could have gone either way – the slime slithered down the walls in both directions. He was so cold that part of him didn't care. He wanted to be out of this river more than anything and even though the tunnel leading off to the right was just as dark and scary as the one they were in, at least it was dry.

'I think we should take the new tunnel,' said James.

'But what if the millipedes went that way?' said Charlie pointing downriver. He stopped and thought for a moment before making up his mind. 'We have to split up.'

'No,' said Billy firmly.

'It's the only way we can be sure we'll find my dad,' insisted Charlie. 'You two take the new tunnel and I'll follow the river and see where it leads.'

Charlie gave Billy the branch. 'There's two of you,' he said. 'Besides, if the river gets any deeper I'll have to start swimming – it won't be much use to me then!'

'Good luck, Charlie,' said Billy taking the branch and pulling himself up the rock face and into the dry tunnel. 'If we find your dad we'll come and get you. You do the same for us. Hopefully we'll see you soon.'

'I hope so too,' said Charlie as he turned away from his two friends and followed the rushing river.

CHAPTER 12

As Charlie splashed down the river without the fire branch, he realised the tunnel wasn't completely dark – strange dull yellowy lights glowed in the walls. Peering at them closely, he saw that they were actually small creatures, the size of his fingernails, which clung to the rock.

'Glow-worms,' whispered Charlie with a smile. 'So I'm not completely alone.' Their light wasn't strong enough to illuminate the darkness, but they did show Charlie which way the tunnel curved and when there

107

was a low-hanging rock or stalactite.

As Charlie waded for what seemed like hours, the smell of dinopoo got stronger and stronger. He wrinkled his nose. It was disgusting.

Suddenly Charlie found the river was moving even faster. He gulped down some stinking air and tried to float along on the surface but it was too rough and he got pulled in and out of the foaming water. Up ahead, the river seemed to disappear all together.

Charlie rubbed his eyes. That couldn't be right. Rivers didn't just disappear. He looked again and gasped in terror. The river didn't disappear – he was heading for a waterfall!

He tried frantically to paddle against the current, but the river was too strong. He kicked out with his

feet hoping they'd snag on something. Nothing. Charlie was heading for the edge of the waterfall and he couldn't do anything about it.

Charlie tried not to think about the height of the waterfall or the rocks that would smash him to pieces when he crashed to the bottom. He'd be over the edge in seconds. Tears welled in his eyes – he'd let his dad down. He took one last gasp of breath, and then felt himself tumbling as he bounced over the waterfall. His arms banged against the rocks, his fingernails scraped against wet stone and his legs were scratched and torn. He was going to be smashed to bits and then . . . and then . . . the air was knocked out of his lungs and slowly Charlie closed his eyes.

Charlie felt like he was in a dream. He knew he

should try to swim but he didn't have the energy to wake himself up. The river had slowed down and the gentle bobbing of the water nudged him into full consciousness.

A terrible smell filled his nostrils. Wearily he opened his eyes. He coughed up a lungful of water and pushed his wet hair out of his face. He tried to stand up but the water was too deep. He trod water while he tried to get his bearings.

He was in a pool at the foot of the waterfall. The river continued on through a smaller tunnel ahead of him. Or at least it tried to, but the small tunnel entrance was clogged with dinopoo. Charlie looked around. He wasn't the only thing bobbing in the pool – there was dinopoo everywhere.

Suddenly, Charlie felt guilty. No wonder the millipedes were angry. If someone had made his home smell like this then he'd be angry too. Charlie had thought that dumping the dinopoo into the underground river would get rid of the problem. Now he realised he'd been wrong. It had got the dinopoo out of Sabreton, but he had just passed the problem on. Charlie shuddered as he remembered the razor-sharp pincers and strange black mouths of the giant millipedes. They might not be very nice but they didn't deserve this.

At that moment, something curled its way under the shoulder strap of his fur skin and Charlie was yanked into the air. Instinctively, he kicked out with his feet, then Charlie turned to look. He screamed. He was face to face with a millipede. It had appeared in a tunnel behind him and it had him gripped in one of its crab-like pincers.

The millipede hissed and bared a pair of lethal-looking fangs at Charlie, before carrying him down the tunnel. Trapped in the millipede's vice-like grip, Charlie began to wish he had drowned in the waterfall after all.

CHAPTER 13

This tunnel was big enough even for the giant millipede to move through. The millipede seemed to ripple along, its legs making a noise like chattering teeth as they clattered against the slimy rock.

Soon the millipede began to slow down. It rounded a corner and opened its mouth. A series of clicks echoed down the tunnel. It was a noise somewhere between the chirping of the crickets around Sabreton on hot summer nights and the noise Charlie's knees made when he'd been sitting cross-legged for too long.

Other clicks answered.

The millipede stopped once they got to a huge cavern. Thousands of glow-worms clung to its walls and ceilings. In the eerie yellow light, Charlie could see many dark tunnels stretching away from the central cavern.

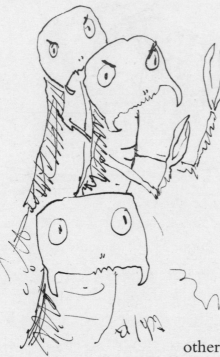

I'm in the heart of the nest, thought Charlie. There was a scuttling sound and a second millipede rippled into the centre of the cavern. Soon a third millipede joined them. The millipedes clicked to each other and touched pincers. One of them looked at Charlie and hissed.

A fourth millipede, bigger than the others and wearing a leaf crown, stalked into the cavern. Charlie recognised him as the leader of the millipedes, the one which had clicked instructions earlier on. In one of its thick pincers was his dad.

Charlie's dad's eyes were closed and his body was slumped. Charlie was too late.

'Dad!' cried Charlie. 'No!'

The large millipede hissed at Charlie to be quiet. Charlie wasn't having any of it.

'Dad!' he cried desperately. 'You've got to wake up! Please!'

The millipede that held Charlie tightened its grip around his stomach. Charlie felt his skin being pinched and the air squeezing out of his lungs.

'Dad!' he gasped.

Charlie's dad coughed and stirred in the grip of the large millipede. Wearily he opened his eyes.

'Dad!' Tears of joy welled up in Charlie's eyes. 'You're alive!'

'Charlie?' mumbled his dad. 'Is that you?'

'Yes!' cried Charlie, laughing with relief. 'I'm here, Dad!'

'I heard your voice. I thought I was dreaming.'

Charlie smiled. He'd got there in time. His dad was OK. Now all they had to do was get out of there.

He turned and looked into the face of the millipede that was holding him so tightly.

'Please!' he gasped. 'Let us go. I didn't mean to ruin your home. I'll put it right. I won't drop dinopoo into your river ever again. Not one lump! I don't care if my dinopants shop has to close. Just let us go! Please!'

The millipede slowly blinked its dull green eyes.

Charlie tried again. 'If you let us go, I'll fix the smell, I promise. Your home will be as good as new in no time.'

The millipede hissed and spat at Charlie. Charlie's hair was instantly covered in thick green gloop.

'It's no use,' said his dad. 'There's no getting through to them. I've tried.'

Clicking filled the air again as the king of the millipedes called out to the others. Suddenly Charlie felt himself being lowered to the ground and the millipede released its grip, but before he could run anywhere it trapped him with its legs, which surrounded him like prison bars. Charlie clutched at them. They were thick and hard and covered in prickly hairs. He shook them. The millipede hissed but its legs didn't budge. Charlie took out his club and bashed it against the legs and the millipede cried out in pain. The leader scuttled over and swiped the club out of Charlie's hands with a spindly leg. It hissed and spat at Charlie and then clicked some more orders. The millipede lifted one of its legs, but it was only so the leader could throw Charlie's dad in the prison with him.

Charlie ran over and hugged him. His dad was weak and tired, but at least he was alive. 'I'm so sorry, Dad!' he cried. 'I'm sorry!'

'You've nothing to be sorry about,' said his dad quietly. 'You were only ever trying to make things better.'

'Well, I've not been very good at that, have I?' said Charlie looking at the millipede legs. He thumped the ground in frustration.

High above them, the millipedes seemed to be talking to each other. Suddenly a fifth millipede swished into the cavern. In its pincers it held Billy and James. Billy was thumping at the pincer with his club and James was shaking with fear.

'Charlie!' gasped Billy in surprise, seeing his friend on the ground.

'Oh no,' moaned James. 'I was hoping *you'd* be the one to rescue *us*!'

The boys landed with a thump as they too were thrown into the makeshift prison.

'What are they doing?' asked Billy, nodding towards the clicking millipedes.

'I think they're deciding what to do with us,' said Charlie's dad.

'Do things like that eat humans?' asked James.

'Remember the cave painting! Things like that eat whatever they can lay their pincers on,' said Charlie quietly. 'What happened to the stick from the fire?' he asked.

'Somebody dropped it in a pile of gloop,' said Billy looking at James.

Suddenly the clicking stopped and the millipede lifted its legs. Charlie's dad and the boys tried to scramble for safety but they soon found themselves trapped against the cold, hard rock.

The king of the millipedes

lowered its head and Charlie looked into its pitch-black mouth. He could see pair after pair of cruel-looking teeth covered in slime. He watched green dribbles of gloop slide down its long fangs and felt them land with a soggy splash on his forehead.

The tip of the fangs were just in front of Charlie's nose now. Charlie realised the millipede was preparing to stab him with them.

Just then, Charlie felt something digging into his thigh. He put his hand into his pocket and felt his fingers curl around his sparking flint. Suddenly he smiled – he'd had an idea.

As the millipede hissed and swooped, Charlie

whipped out his sparking flint and struck it against the cavern wall. Sparks blazed in the dull cave. The millipede recoiled in horror, his green eyes blinking in panic, dazzled by the light. Charlie struck the wall again and more sparks filled the cavern. The other millipedes cowered away. They were obviously terrified.

'They don't like that, Charlie!' said Billy reaching into his pocket for his own flint.

'I know,' replied Charlie. 'It's so dark down here I don't think their eyes are used to the bright light.'

Billy struck his flint against the wall too and soon James was doing the same. The millipedes, temporarily blinded, stumbled into each other as they rubbed at their eyes with their pincers. In the confusion, they got tangled in each others' legs.

'Now's our chance!' shouted Charlie. 'Run!' The three boys and Charlie's dad ran towards the tunnels.

'Use the one that Billy and James came through!' yelled Charlie. 'There was a waterfall in mine.'

Billy led the way, sparking his flint against the wall as he went.

He stopped to pick up his club and tucked it back inside his fur skin and Charlie did the same.

'Come on!' called Charlie. 'We've got to get out.'

CHAPTER 14

They pounded down the tunnel towards the river, sparking their flints all the time. Charlie's dad even managed to find the flint that he had made many years ago, buried in one of the pockets of his fur skin, and joined in.

Behind them they could hear the scuttling sound of millipede legs.

'Their eyes must be getting used to the sparks,' said Billy.

They all ran even faster, but in his haste, Charlie's dad skidded on some loose gravel and tumbled on to the hard ground. He cried out. Charlie winced as he looked at his dad's ankle – it was red and swelling up fast.

'Come on, Dad!' hissed Charlie. 'We have to go! They're getting closer!'

Charlie's dad tried to stand, but he fell down again in pain – his ankle was twisted.

'You go, Charlie,' he said. 'I'll slow you down.'

'No!' yelled Charlie. 'You're coming with us!'

'Charlie,' said James, nodding back up the tunnel, where they could see the king of the millipedes spitting gloop as he scuttled towards them.

James jumped between the millipede and Charlie's dad, and showered the tunnel with sparks. The millipede recoiled only briefly, but it gave Billy the time he needed. He bent down and pulled Charlie's dad to his feet and supported him as he hobbled towards the river, while Charlie and James unleashed another shower of sparks before following.

At the river, Billy jumped straight into the fast water before helping Charlie's dad down. Charlie and James were close behind. Together they half carried and half dragged Charlie's dad up the river that would eventually lead to the dinoloo holes.

They could hear the millipedes splashing into the water behind them. They were gaining on them – they had a lot more legs and they were used to walking in the river. It was very difficult for the boys to make any progress at all as they struggled against the river's current, and having to support Charlie's dad made things even worse.

'Leave me here. I'm only slowing you down,' hissed Charlie's dad again.

Charlie looked at his father and bit his lip. He couldn't leave him to the millipedes. But he was right – they weren't moving fast enough.

James struck his flint against the tunnel wall, but the wall was too damp for sparks.

'What do we do, Charlie?' he asked, his eyes wide with terror as the millipedes came towards them.

Suddenly they heard a loud splash further up the river. One of the millipedes must have used another tunnel to get ahead of them. They were surrounded! Charlie pulled out his club, ran towards the splashing sound and yelled. He wasn't going down without a fight.

But when he saw what had caused the splash he nearly dropped his club in surprise.

'Steggy!' he gasped. 'What are you doing here?'

Steggy gave Charlie a sheepish grin.

'Billy! Help me get Dad on to Steggy's back!' Charlie yelled.

Together they heaved Charlie's dad on to Steggy's lowered back and, as he clung on for dear life, the boys and Steggy hurried as fast as they could up-river.

Eventually, Steggy and Charlie's dad were standing under the dinoloo holes. Sunlight streamed through the openings on to the rippling water. The boys had been underground all night! They came to a halt next to Steggy.

'Well?' gasped Charlie. 'What are we waiting for?'

Charlie's dad tugged at the vine rope that still dangled into the hole. It snapped in his hand and splashed into the water.

'Now what?' he asked.

Charlie looked in horror. He had absolutely no idea how to get out. They were stuck! They could only look on helplessly as the millipedes advanced.

CHAPTER 15

An ear-splitting screech filled the air. It was part lion's roar and part raven's caw and it echoed all around. The millipedes stopped dead in their tracks.

Above them the ceiling began to crack and crumble. What was happening?

Charlie and the others ducked out of the way of a falling rock and crouched against the tunnel wall for cover. Something seemed to be smashing its way through the largest of the dinoloo holes – it was a huge tail! The hole got bigger and bigger, until eventually a mighty foot splashed into the underground river and sent a wave of icy water towards the millipedes. They

backed away as a second foot joined the first, and the
T. Rex landed with a massive splash.

The T. Rex looked around searching for Charlie and
his friends. When he found them he leaned over and
plucked them one by one from the tunnel with his
teeth, and lifted them gently up on to the ground
beside the broken remains of the dinoloos. Finally he
grabbed Steggy by the neck and lifted him and
Charlie's dad to safety too. Then he turned and roared
at the millipedes, flashing his terrifying teeth, his eyes
glinting with fury.

The millipedes scuttled away in terror. Nobody messed with the T. Rex.

On the surface, Charlie, his dad and his friends were amazed to find the mayor, Boris and Barry Relic racing towards them on Barry's triceratops, Teresa, followed by loads of different dinosaurs.

'Every dinosaur in Sabreton must be coming here,' gasped James.

'We thought you might need reinforcements!' called Barry with a toothless smile.

'When your father didn't come back last night

your mother got worried,' explained the mayor, jumping down from Teresa. 'She came to see me. We decided to marshall the troops and come and help. When the dinosaurs found out it was you, they fell over themselves to help. Some of them even managed to persuade the T. Rex to come too! Steggy insisted on going on ahead in case we were too late. I wonder where he gets that impatience from?' The mayor winked at Charlie.

Below the ground, the T. Rex was roaring and stamping and swishing his tail against the side of the cave. Steggy ran to the dinoloo holes and began to stamp and bash the ground around them, encouraging all the other dinosaurs to join in.

In the tunnel, the millipedes were showered with falling rocks raining from the ceiling like hailstones. The millipedes protected themselves with their giant pincers as they turned and ran back towards their nest.

But the T. Rex continued to roar and swipe its massive tail at the cave walls, sending tremors through the earth, causing larger rocks to crack and mighty stalactites to fall.

'They're causing a landslide,' gasped Charlie.

Huge, thick clouds of dust filled the air as the dinosaurs stamped and stomped until, with a giant crack, the ground gave way.

Finally, there was quiet. Once the dust had settled, Charlie opened his eyes. The T. Rex was standing where the dinoloos had been. The ground had tumbled into the river forming a slope that blocked the wide tunnel. The water flowed underneath but there was no way a dinosaur could get through or a millipede could get out. The T. Rex lifted one last boulder and heaped it on top of the others with a growl.

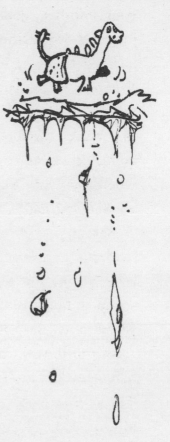

Charlie clambered down to where a pincer was poking out from between the rocks. The T. Rex growled and swiped at it with a claw.

'No!' cried Charlie. 'Don't!'

The T. Rex looked at Charlie and shrugged his shoulders. He'd never understand humans. Charlie reached out his hand and gently shook the pincer.

'I'm sorry,' he called, 'I didn't

mean for any of this to happen.'

The pincer disappeared through the landslide. From somewhere deep under the earth Charlie heard a hiss and a click as the millipede scuttled away.

Charlie looked at the T. Rex and then at his dad. 'I guess we're free,' he said with a smile.

The T. Rex growled and turned to begin the long climb back up to the top of his mountain.

'Come on,' said Billy taking Charlie by the arm. 'Let's go home.'

And slowly the dinosaurs and humans made their way back to Sabreton.

CHAPTER 16

One week later, Charlie and his friends were standing by the landslide waiting for the mayor to arrive to open their rebuilt dinoloos.

'I don't get it,' said James shaking his head. 'We get attacked by giant millipedes, we almost drown, we're nearly killed by falling rocks and you still want to open a dinoloo!'

Charlie smiled. His mum had smothered him in kisses when they'd got back to Sabreton and then she'd told his dad off for being stupid enough to get captured by giant millipedes in the first place. Charlie and his friends had been awarded the Sabreton medal of honour for being brave enough to rescue Charlie's dad. The only downside to everything was that the mayor still wanted to close the dinopants shop. Now that the dinoloos were no more, the dinopoo problem was back with a vengeance.

Charlie had been very upset, but he had managed to persuade the mayor to give his dinoloos one last chance with a very minor alteration. Charlie didn't want to move the dinopoo problem on for others to deal with again, but he thought he might have come up with a solution that would make everybody happy.

He and his friends worked long and hard once more until the dinoloos were rebuilt and ready for use.

'I don't get it either,' said Billy as he looked at the dinoloos. 'They're just the same as before.'

'Yeah,' agreed James, 'but with the millipedes blocked under the ground I suppose we can put the dinopoo into the river and not worry about it.'

'No!' said Charlie. 'We can't do that! I'm not polluting anything ever again.'

'So what are you going to do with all the dinopoo?'

Just then the sound of a trumpet filled the air and Boris and the mayor trotted into view.

'Are we ready, Charlie?' called the mayor.

'Nearly,' said Charlie. 'There's just one last thing to do. Dad!'

Charlie's dad limped out of his little booth. His ankle was heavily bandaged but he was still smiling. He was wearing his dinoloo attendant's uniform. He whistled and Teresa and Barry Relic appeared from behind one of the dinoloos. Teresa was pulling three huge rolls of stretched animal hides behind her.

'I hope this works, Charlie,' called Barry with a smile.

'It will,' said Charlie. 'Trust me.'

Charlie's dad unrolled one of the sheets. It was massive.

'What's that for?' asked James.

'We hang it in the river tunnel under a dinoloo hole,' said Charlie. 'That way we catch the dinopoo before it splashes into the river.'

'I still don't understand,' said Billy scratching his head. 'It doesn't solve the problem, it just means we've got a load of dinopoo in a sheet. Who'd want that?'

'We would,' said a little man with a thin straggly beard, carrying a spade. Behind him were ten other men all carrying different farmyard tools.

'Farmers?' gasped James. 'What

are they going to do with it?'

'Do you remember how the poo made all the flowers in Dinopoo Field grow?' asked Charlie. 'Well, imagine what it will do to the farmers' crops!'

James and Billy thought for a moment and then smiled.

'We'll have a huge harvest in no time!' nodded the farmer. 'All we have to do is dry the dinopoo out in our fields so that it loses its smell and then spread it on the crops. We'll all be eating mammoth-size fruit and vegetables come harvest time!'

'Brilliant!' said James, patting Charlie on the back.

'I thought so,' said the mayor bristling his moustache. Even Boris managed to smile.

They all helped stretch a sheet under each of the dinoloo holes. The sheets had loops of vine rope in every corner, and they hooked the loops over wooden pegs which Charlie had driven into the ground around the dinoloos. The sheets hung under the holes like hammocks.

Once they had finished, Charlie looked at the dinoloos proudly. They were back and they were better than ever!

From that day on, the dinopoo was spread on the fields of Sabreton and it made all the crops grow better than ever before. The town had a bumper harvest when the autumn came and, best of all, Charlie and his friends still got to make dinopants in the dinopants shop. James bought himself three pterodactyl-skin tunics with the precious stones he was given for his work and Billy bought every stick of liquorice in town and ate them all without once getting sick. Charlie's dad wore his attendant's uniform proudly each day and loved his job.

Every once in a while, when he wasn't too busy in his dinopants shop, Charlie would find himself sitting in The Hungry Bone Café munching on an enormous banana. Thanks to the dinoloos, bananas were now three times bigger than they used to be. The only person complaining was Peter Tray. His plates were heavier than ever and he puffed and panted his way around the café tables. Charlie didn't mind though – he thought one worn out waiter was a price worth paying for his magnificent dinoloos.